ASTRID & APOLLO

AND THE
SUPER STAYCATION

BY
V.T. BIDANIA

ILLUSTRATED BY
EVELT YANAIT

PICTURE WINDOW BOOKS
a capstone imprint

To Mom & Dad, grateful for the many vacations we had together —VTB

Published by Picture Window Books,
an imprint of Capstone.
1710 Roe Crest Drive
North Mankato, Minnesota 56003
capstonepub.com

Library of Congress Cataloging-in-Publication Data
Names: Bidania, V. T., author. | Yanait, Evelt, illustrator.
Title: Astrid and Apollo and the super staycation / by V.T. Bidania ; illustrated by Evelt Yanait.
Description: North Mankato, Minnesota : Picture Window Books, [2022] | Series: Astrid and Apollo | Audience: Ages 6-8. | Audience: Grades K-1. | Summary: When bad weather cancels the family trip to Laos, where their mother's cousin is getting married, twins Astrid and Apollo try to cheer up their parents by surprising them with a Laos-themed stay-at-home vacation.
Identifiers: LCCN 2021970041 (print) | LCCN 2021970042 (ebook) | ISBN 9781666337457 (hardcover) | ISBN 9781666337419 (paperback) | ISBN 9781666337525 (pdf)
Subjects: LCSH: Hmong American families—Juvenile fiction. | Twins—Juvenile fiction. | Brothers and sisters—Juvenile fiction. | Family vacations—Juvenile fiction. | Parent and child—Juvenile fiction. | CYAC: Twins—Fiction. | Brothers and sisters—Fiction. | Family vacations—Fiction. | Parent and child—Fiction. | Hmong American families—Fiction. | LCGFT: Picture books.
Classification: LCC PZ7.1.B5333 Ate 2022 (print) | LCC PZ7.1.B5333 (ebook) | DDC [E]—dc23
LC record available at https://lccn.loc.gov/2021970041
LC ebook record available at https://lccn.loc.gov/2021970042

Designer: Tracy Davies

Design Elements: Shutterstock/Ingo Menhard, 60, Shutterstock/Yangxiong (Hmong pattern), 5 and throughout

Printed and bound in the USA. 4882

Table of Contents

ASTRID GAO NOU

Hi, I'm Astrid. My twin brother is Apollo, and we were born in Minnesota. We live here with our mom, dad, and little sister, Eliana.

Hi, I'm Apollo! Our mom and dad were both born in Laos. They came to the United States when they were very young and grew up here.

APOLLO NOU KOU

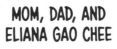

MOM, DAD, AND ELIANA GAO CHEE

HMONG WORDS

gao (GOW)—girl; it is often placed in front of a girl's name. Hmong spelling: *nkauj*

Gao Chee (GOW chee)—shiny girl. Hmong spelling: *Nkauj Ci*

Gao Hlee (GOW lee)—moon girl. Hmong spelling: *Nkauj Hli*

Gao Nou (GOW new)—sun girl. Hmong spelling: *Nkauj Hnub*

Hmong (MONG)—a group of people who came to the U.S. from Laos. Many Hmong from Laos now live in Minnesota. Hmong spelling: *Hmoob*

Nia Thy (nee-YAH thy)—grandmother on the mother's side. Hmong spelling: *Niam Tais*

Nou Kou (NEW koo)—star. Hmong spelling: *Hnub Qub*

tou (TOO)—boy or son; it is often placed in front of a boy's name. Hmong spelling: *tub*

CHAPTER 1

Oh No!

"Eliana, be careful with your paint!" said Astrid. "You are splashing red paint onto my green grass."

Apollo moved his painting away. "You're getting it in my blue river too! The paint's all over your hands."

Eliana made a face.

"We are using paintbrushes, but *you* are supposed to be finger painting, not *hand* painting," Astrid said.

Their dog, Luna, sat near the newspaper covering the floor, watching them. Eliana shook her hands in the air.

"Don't get paint on Luna!" said Apollo.

"Paint, paint, PAINT!" Eliana yelled.

Her hands were covered in red paint. She had red fingerprints on her arms. Red handprints were splattered on her paint smock.

Astrid and Apollo picked up their paintings and moved to the other side of the coffee table. Luna followed them.

"Kids, why are you still painting? We're leaving in two days. You should be packing!" Dad said. He was carrying a big suitcase down the stairs.

"Dad, we finished packing yesterday," said Astrid.

"Don't you remember? Look," Apollo said.

He pointed at the neat row of suitcases in the living room. One medium green suitcase for Apollo. One medium blue suitcase for Astrid. And one small purple suitcase for Eliana.

"That's right!" Dad said. "We've been so busy, I forgot. I still can't believe we're going back to Laos after all this time."

"Are you excited for the trip, Dad?" Astrid asked.

Luna hurried over to Dad, and he picked her up.

"Yes! It's been many years since we left Laos. Your mom's excited too. She's looking forward to her cousin's wedding. And she can't wait to see her grandparents again."

"Me too!" Astrid and Apollo said at the same time.

"Me too!" said Eliana. She made two fists and smacked them on top of her painting on the table. *Splat!*

"Eliana, look what you did!" Apollo picked up Eliana's painting. Bright red fist prints were now on the top of the white paper.

"Eliana, can you please listen to Dad?" Astrid said. She turned to him. "Tell us your favorite thing about Laos, Dad."

"I was too young. I don't remember a lot, but I know I miss the food. I miss the river by my house. I liked playing in that river." Dad smiled.

"Did you see any fish in there?" said Astrid.

"I forget. Maybe," Dad said.

"Will you take us there?" Apollo asked.

Dad nodded. "I don't know if we can find that one, but we'll try to visit as many rivers as we can."

Astrid and Apollo smiled at each other. "Yes!" they said together.

"YES!" Eliana screamed.

That's when they heard Mom exclaim, "Oh no!"

CHAPTER 2

Fifty Years

"What happened?" Apollo wondered out loud.

Astrid and Apollo ran with Dad into the kitchen. Eliana and Luna followed them. They found Mom sitting at the table, staring at her computer.

"What's wrong?" Dad asked.

Mom put her hand on her head. "Our trip to Laos is ruined! The airline delayed our flights."

"Why?" said Astrid.

"We're supposed to fly to California the day after tomorrow. From there, we fly to Japan, and then Laos. But there's a very bad storm coming, so now our flights are delayed," Mom said.

"How long do we have to wait?" asked Apollo.

"I'm not sure. But if we don't leave on time, we'll be late getting to Laos. That means we could miss the wedding!"

Astrid moved closer to Mom. "Is there another flight we can take?"

Mom pointed at her computer. On the screen was a map with a giant purple cloud covering the top part of the United States.

"The storm is moving to all the big cities with airports. Then it will create more storms. I don't think we'll be able to fly anywhere for days," she said.

Astrid read the computer screen. "*Worst storms in fifty years.* Wow."

"Fifty years?" said Apollo.

"Fif-tee ears?" echoed Eliana from across the room.

Dad put his arm around Mom. "Don't worry. We'll figure it out," he said.

"Let me call the airline now and check." Mom stood and picked up her phone.

As she walked out of the room, Astrid and Apollo frowned.

"Mom looks so worried and sad," said Apollo.

Astrid shook her head. "I don't want her to be sad."

Dad sighed. "Let's see what they say. Maybe the weather will get better, and everything will be okay."

"Oh-kay," Eliana said and turned to Dad for a hug.

"Don't!" Astrid said, but it was too late. Dad's sweater now had red handprints all over the front.

* * *

When Mom got off the phone, she looked even sadder. "They said planes can't fly for a couple of days. We have to wait until the storms clear. They don't know when that will be."

"But we'll still go, right?" said Apollo.

"I don't know. It's a very bad storm. If we do go, we won't make it to the wedding," Mom said, shaking her head in disappointment.

Astrid hugged Mom. "I'm sorry, Mom."

Mom kissed Astrid's head. "Thank you, Astrid. I'm going to call my grandma now and let her know what's happening."

After Mom left the room, Apollo said, "Dad, can we go to Laos even if we miss the wedding?"

Dad read the news on the computer. "I'm not sure. We might have to cancel this trip."

"What?" Astrid said in surprise. "But why?"

"It takes long to travel this far. Even if we leave a few days from now, once we get there, it will be almost time to come back. We won't have enough time to enjoy our stay," Dad explained.

Apollo made a face. "But can't we just stay longer?"

"I wish we could, but Mom and I have to get back to work. We can't take any more time off," said Dad.

Astrid sat down on a chair. "This is not good. Mom was so excited for this trip. She's been planning it for a long time!"

"You too, Dad! You were going to show us the rivers," said Apollo.

Dad shook his head. "This is very disappointing, but planes can't fly in this weather. There's nothing we can do. I'm sorry, kids."

Dad looked at the paint on his sweater and Eliana's hands. "Let's get cleaned up." He and Eliana walked out of the kitchen.

While Mom talked on the phone with her grandmother, Astrid and Apollo looked at photos spread out on the kitchen table.

"Nia Thy brought these yesterday. She couldn't take this trip with us, so she wanted to show us these pictures," said Astrid.

"I remember. She said they show Mom's favorite things about Laos," said Apollo.

"Look at this field of red flowers," Astrid said.

Apollo nodded. "Mom says those are called poppy flowers. She played there with her sisters."

"Look at this one of her grandma and grandpa farming," said Astrid. "Mom loves Nia Thy's stories about farming. Just like Dad loves stories about his family farm."

Apollo passed her a picture. "Here's Mom's family eating. Looks yummy!"

"See her grandma cooking behind them? She's smashing something into a bowl," said Astrid.

Astrid and Apollo both grinned and said, "Papaya salad!"

"Look here," said Astrid. "Mom's so small. She's wearing cute red flip-flops. She talks about these shoes all the time."

"Dad had shoes like that too!" Apollo said.

He pointed to a framed picture of Dad on the wall. It was taken when he was a little kid in Laos. He was wearing blue flip-flops.

The twins smiled.

Then Apollo put the pictures down. "I really hope we can still go on this trip. It will make Mom and Dad so happy."

Astrid rubbed at a drop of paint on her arm. "But in case we can't go, we have to come up with a way to cheer them up."

Apollo nodded. "This was supposed to be a fun vacation. Now we have to stay home."

Astrid clapped her hands. "We can still have fun. We can have a *staycation*—a vacation at home!"

Apollo's eyes grew wide. "That's right. We can take Mom and Dad to Laos, right here! We will surprise them."

"Staycation surprise!" they said and laughed.

CHAPTER 3

Brainstorming

Astrid and Apollo got to work on their surprise right away.

"First, let's think about how to do the staycation. What can we do to make Mom and Dad feel like they're in Laos?" said Apollo.

"Let's brainstorm," Astrid said. She took a pencil and notepad from a drawer and wrote down WHAT M&D LOVE ABOUT LAOS.

"We'll make a list," she said.

"We know Dad likes rivers. Can you write down rivers?" asked Apollo.

"Yes, and we know Mom loves the poppy fields with red flowers. I'll write down poppy fields too," Astrid said.

Apollo sat down at the table. "Mom liked her grandparents' stories about the farm. Dad liked the farm too. Can you add farming?"

Astrid nodded. "Now we have three things. Do we need more?"

Apollo looked at the pictures again. "Flip-flops! They both wore fun flip-flops."

"Yes! I will add flip-flops to the list. Anything else?" Astrid tapped the pencil to her chin.

Apollo saw the picture of Mom eating. "What about food?"

"They both love papaya salad," Astrid said wrote that down. Then she read the whole list. "We have *rivers, poppy fields, farming, flip-flops,* and *papaya salad.* What do we do now?"

They thought for a moment. Then Apollo looked at the paper that Eliana had slammed her fists down on.

"Hey—Eliana's red fist prints look like poppy flowers!" he said. "What if we make paintings of poppies? We can use green paint for the field. Then we can have Eliana make red fist prints for the flowers!"

"Her fist prints *do* look like poppy flowers!" Astrid wrote HOW TO BRING LAOS HOME and wrote *poppy field painting* underneath it.

"And we can paint a long river for Dad," Apollo said.

"He'll like that!" Astrid wrote *river painting* on the list.

"I know!" said Apollo. "For papaya salad, we can ask Auntie May to make some and bring it here. Her papaya salad's the best!"

"Good idea! But let's not make it too spicy." Astrid added *papaya salad – NOT SPICY* to the list.

"What else?" said Apollo.

Astrid said, "Auntie May lives close to Hmong Village. I can ask her and Lily to pick up flip-flops for all of us."

She wrote down *flip-flops from Auntie May.*

"Great! Last of all, farming. What can we do for farming?" said Apollo.

Astrid thought for a minute. "What if we ask Nia Thy and Uncle Meng to bring over Hmong farming tools?"

Apollo nodded. "Yes! They have a lot of tools. We could ask them to bring fruits and vegetables too. This will remind Mom and Dad about Hmong farming."

"Yay!" said Astrid. She wrote *farm tools, fruits and veggies.*

"Now let's call everyone for help. Then tomorrow we can make the paintings," said Astrid.

Apollo nodded. "You want to call Auntie May and Lily? I'll call Nia Thy and Uncle Meng."

"Okay!" said Astrid.

* * *

After the twins had borrowed their parents' phones, they handed them back.

"Thank you for letting us play Boogies Bugs," said Apollo, even though they hadn't really played the game app. They had taken the phones to their rooms to make phone calls to their relatives.

"Yes, that's our favorite game," said Astrid, trying not to smile so her parents wouldn't suspect anything.

But they were too busy looking at the computer to notice.

"You're welcome," Dad murmured as he scratched his forehead.

"Well, for sure we won't be taking this trip, kids." Mom sighed and pointed at the computer.

Astrid and Apollo opened their eyes wide as they read the words on the screen: *Flights around the world canceled for the next week.*

* * *

The next day, Mom and Dad unpacked the suitcases.

"We'll be upstairs putting clothes away," Dad said.

"Can you stay up there for a while?" asked Apollo.

Astrid thought fast to come up with an excuse. "We want to paint, and Mom doesn't like the smell," she explained.

Mom nodded. "Open the windows a little and try not to make a mess."

As soon as they left, Apollo said, "Get ready, Eliana. You can make your red fist prints!"

Eliana looked at her fists.

"It's okay. We *want* you to make red fist prints this time," said Astrid.

Eliana smiled. She swung her elbows and shook from side to side in a little happy dance.

Apollo ripped off paper from his big painting pad. "Let's do a lot of poppy flower paintings. I need paper for a river too. Is five pieces enough?"

"Five is great. We can tape the pieces together." Astrid handed him tape from their art supplies.

Apollo said, "This will be a very long river!"

"Long!" yelled Eliana.

"Eliana, we have to be quiet." Apollo put his finger to his lips. "Can you whisper?"

"YES!" Eliana screamed.

"Shh," said Astrid. "We don't want Mom and Dad to know about our surprise."

"Suh-pies!" Eliana whispered loudly as she jumped up and down.

CHAPTER 4

Human Paintbrush

Astrid picked up a paintbrush and opened different green paints. She dipped the brush in the paint and painted tall grass in several shades of green. Then she painted long stems and leaves for the poppy flowers.

"Your turn, Eliana," she whispered and pointed to the top of the stems. "Remember when you put red paint on your hands? Do it again and press your fists here."

Eliana nodded happily.

While Astrid and Eliana made the poppy flowers, Apollo painted a long, winding river. He used a big paintbrush and bright blue paint.

He started at one end and painted across the paper. He wiggled his arm up and down so the water would be wavy like a real river.

"This is long!" he said as he painted from one side of the paper to the other.

"Maybe it's the longest river in Laos!" said Astrid.

When Apollo was done, he painted grass and rocks near the edges of the river.

"That looks nice!" said Astrid. "But I feel like something's missing."

Apollo stepped back and looked at his painting. "Me too. What could we add?"

Eliana squinted at the water. "Fish!" she said.

Astrid and Apollo smiled at each other.

"Of course! Thanks, Eliana," said Apollo. "Do you want to paint fish?"

Eliana nodded.

"But her hands have red paint," said Astrid. "She needs to wash them first."

Apollo smiled. "What if she uses her *feet* to paint?" he said.

"Feet?" Eliana and Astrid both said at once, and then all three laughed.

Apollo put more newspaper on the floor and then set his river painting down on top of it. Next he poured a shiny silvery paint into a puddle. Then he and Astrid helped Eliana step in the paint and then onto the river painting.

Eliana giggled and pressed down with her feet and toes. She was painting silver fish!

"You are a human paintbrush!" said Apollo.

Then Luna tried to jump onto the river painting, but Astrid picked her up before she could smudge the fish prints.

"We said human paintbrush, not puppy paintbrush!" Astrid said.

When the paintings were done, the twins cleaned up their art supplies. They put their paint smocks away and carried Eliana to the bathroom so she wouldn't leave paint footprints on the floor.

Luna chased them into the bathroom as they cleaned up. She watched them wash paint off Eliana's feet.

Astrid blew a big bubble from her soapy hands. Eliana popped it with her finger. Apollo blew a bubble too. It floated to the floor.

Luna stared at the bubble as it landed on her nose. Then she sneezed!

They dried their hands and walked back into the living room. Astrid said, "Where should we hide the paintings?"

Apollo looked around. "How about behind the couch? We'll tell Mom and Dad not to peek there."

The twins pulled the couch away from the wall. They were hiding the paintings on the floor behind the couch just as Mom and Dad walked in.

Mom looked at the room. "Why is the couch moved away from the wall?"

"No reason! Don't worry, we didn't spill anything," Astrid said quickly.

"Actually, we planned a surprise for tomorrow," Apollo said.

Dad leaned his head to one side. "What kind of surprise?"

"You have to wait until tomorrow to find out," Astrid said.

Apollo nodded. "You'll see in the morning!"

"Okay," Mom said with a small smile. "Let's have lunch now. Since we aren't going to the airport tomorrow, we can figure out what to do instead."

Astrid and Apollo saw the sad look on Mom's face.

Dad saw it too. "At least we don't have to get up early. We can all sleep in!" he said cheerily.

Astrid and Apollo nodded. They felt bad for Mom, but they were also excited for the staycation surprise. They knew they wouldn't be sleeping in!

CHAPTER 5

Staycation Surprise!

The next morning, Astrid woke up first. Outside the window, she could see big clouds in the sky. The worst storm in fifty years was starting.

Eliana was still asleep, so Astrid quietly climbed out of bed. She walked down the hall to Apollo's room and knocked on the door.

"Apollo?" she whispered. "Wake up so we can get the surprise ready! I told everyone to come over early."

"I'm up!" he said and opened the door. He had a big grin on his face.

Astrid and Apollo tiptoed down the stairs. Luna was already awake in her kennel. She was sitting up and watching them with big eyes. She was ready for the surprise too!

"Good morning, Luna." Astrid opened the kennel and Luna hopped out, wagging her tail.

Luna hurried over to the paintings and sniffed them.

Apollo leaned over to check them. "They're all dry now. They turned out so good!"

Astrid looked at the paintings. "The colors are bright! Eliana's poppy flowers and fish look perfect."

Apollo nodded. "Let's hang them up!"

Together, the twins taped the paintings all over the room. They put a field of poppy flowers on each wall. Then they hung the river painting on the longest wall.

Astrid looked around. "It's like we're really outside!"

"Like we're really in Laos!" Apollo said.

"Wow!" said Eliana.

Astrid and Apollo turned to see her coming down the stairs.

"Pretty, right?" asked Astrid.

Eliana nodded and curled up on the couch with her blanket. Luna hopped up beside her.

Apollo looked out the window.

It was starting to rain. "Uncle Meng's van is here! And I see Auntie May parking. There's Lily coming up the sidewalk with her umbrella. Everyone's here!"

Astrid opened the front door. "Quick, come in out of the rain! Let's get everything ready before Mom and Dad wake up!"

* * *

"Mom? Dad? Time for your surprise!" Astrid said through her parents' bedroom door.

Apollo knocked on it three times. "Come downstairs to see!"

"What is it?" said Mom in a sleepy voice.

They could hear Dad yawning.

"I thought we were sleeping in today?" he said.

"Come down!" said Apollo. "This is better than sleep!"

He and Astrid hurried to the living room. They were so excited they couldn't stop giggling.

When Mom and Dad got downstairs, they were surprised to see Nia Thy, Uncle Meng, Auntie May, and Lily all in the living room.

"Surprise!" the whole group yelled.

"Well this is a surprise! And why is everyone here?" Mom asked with a laugh.

Dad rubbed his eyes. "And so early too."

Mom covered her mouth with her hands. "What are these wonderful paintings on the walls?"

Nia Thy nodded at Astrid and Apollo. They stood up.

"Welcome to your staycation surprise!" Astrid and Apollo said.

Eliana waved her arm out. "Da-da!" she said.

Astrid took Mom's hand and walked her to one of the poppy paintings. "Here are your poppy flowers from when you were little."

Mom put a hand over her heart. Her eyes watered. "They're beautiful."

Apollo took Dad to the river painting. "And here is the river you played in as a kid."

Dad smiled and nodded. "And I even see fish in there! Little . . . feet-shaped fish?"

"*I* did it!" said Eliana and pointed at her toes for all to see.

"This is terrific," said Dad.

"Now, come over here," said Astrid. She took her parents to the coffee table where there were bowls of fresh fruits and vegetables. Beside the table was a Hmong shovel, an ax, and a hoe.

"This is to remind you of farming in Laos," said Apollo.

Mom and Dad looked at the tools.

Nia Thy smiled. "Just like back home."

Then Astrid said, "You even get to eat your favorite food from Laos!"

Auntie May walked over and handed them a big bowl of papaya salad.

"For breakfast?" Dad asked.

Mom smelled the bowl. "Mmm. I can smell the shrimp paste. And the pepper."

Luna stood by Mom and wiggled her nose.

"So can Luna!" Uncle Meng chuckled.

Auntie May handed them each a fork. "Try some."

"Wait!" said Lily. "You have to wear these first."

She gave pairs of flip-flops to the whole family. Mom and Dad laughed as they slipped on the shoes.

Then Astrid said, "Mom and Dad, we know you're sad we couldn't go to Laos today."

"We're sad too," Apollo said. "But even though we couldn't have a vacation there, we can still have a *staycation* right here."

"We brought Laos to you!" said Astrid.

Mom and Dad hugged the twins and Eliana.

Astrid pointed all around the room. "Well?"

"Do you like it?" Apollo asked.

Mom and Dad looked at each other and smiled.

"No." Dad shook his head. "We love it!"

"Thank you very much! This feels just like home," Mom said.

The wind howled outside and rain tapped against the windows of the house. The storm was here. But Astrid, Apollo, and their family enjoyed their Laos staycation safe at home.

- Hmong people first lived in southern China. Many of them moved to Southeast Asia in the 1800s. Some Hmong decided to stay in the country of Laos (pronounced *LAH-ohs).*

LAOS

- In the 1950s, a war called the Vietnam War started in Southeast Asia. The United States joined this war. They asked the Hmong in Laos to help them. When the U.S. lost the war, Hmong people had to leave Laos.

- After 1975, many Hmong came to the U.S. as refugees. Refugees are people who escape from their country to find a new, safe place to live. Today, Minnesota is home to around 80,000 Hmong.

- Many Hmong American families enjoy outdoor activities like camping, boating, and fishing.

banh mi—a spicy sandwich filled with meat and pickled vegetables

bubble tea—a sweet dessert drink that comes in different flavors and has chewy black balls made of tapioca

fish sauce—a strong, salty sauce that is used as a seasoning for Hmong and other Southeast Asian dishes

pandan—a tropical plant used as a sweet flavoring in Southeast Asian cakes and desserts

papaya salad—a sour, spicy salad made of papaya (that is not yet ripe), tomatoes, garlic, lime, shrimp paste, fish sauce, and fresh pepper

peanut sauce—a creamy sweet and spicy peanut dip that is eaten with spring rolls

pork and green vegetable soup—pork and leafy green vegetables boiled in a broth

spring roll—fresh vegetables, cooked rice noodles, and meat wrapped in soft rice paper. Spring rolls are different from egg rolls because they are not fried.

Vietnamese coffee—rich coffee served with sweetened condensed milk

GLOSSARY

brainstorm (BRAYN-storm)—to come up with many ideas

cancel (KAN-suhl)—to stop or end something before it begins

delay (dih-LAY)—to put off until a later time

hoe (HOE)—a tool with a thin flat blade on a long handle used for gardening or farming

kennel (KEN-uhl)—a small enclosure for a pet

poppy (POP-ee)—a flower usually reddish orange in color

smudge (SMUDJ)—to smear

staycation (stay-KAY-shun)—a vacation taken at home or in your home city

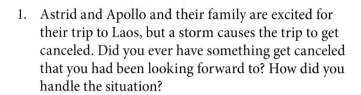
1. Astrid and Apollo and their family are excited for their trip to Laos, but a storm causes the trip to get canceled. Did you ever have something get canceled that you had been looking forward to? How did you handle the situation?

2. Astrid and Apollo know their parents are especially sad about missing the trip to Laos. What clues in the text let the reader know how important their home country is to their mom and dad?

3. Think about a time someone did something nice to cheer you up. Did it work? Was there ever a time when you tried to cheer someone up? What did you do?

WRITE IT DOWN

1. Sometimes decisions are out of our control, such as when bad weather affects our plans. Draw a picture of how you feel when something is beyond your control.

2. Imagine that Astrid and Apollo's trip to Laos had not been canceled. Write a paragraph describing some of the things they might have done there, based on what you read in the story.

3. What would you like to do for a staycation? Would you visit a local museum? A park? Maybe you would have a theme party, like Astrid and Apollo did. Make a list or draw pictures of five things you would like to do with your family if you took a staycation.

ABOUT THE AUTHOR

V.T. Bidania has been writing stories ever since she was five years old. She was born in Laos and grew up in St. Paul, Minnesota, right where Astrid and Apollo live! She has an MFA in creative writing from The New School and is a McKnight Writing Fellow. She lives outside of the Twin Cities and spends her free time reading all the books she can find, writing more stories, and playing with her family's sweet Morkie.

ABOUT THE ILLUSTRATOR

Evelt Yanait is a freelance children's digital artist from Barcelona, Spain, where she grew up drawing and reading wonderful illustrated books. After working as a journalist for an NGO for many years, she decided to focus on illustration, her true passion. She loves to learn, write, travel, and watch documentaries, discovering and capturing new lifestyles and stories whenever she can. She also does social work with children and youth, and she's currently earning a Social Education degree.